THE MAGIC CHAN
A PANDIT AND HIS PUPIL WERE ONCE PASSING THROUGH A FOREST.
SUDDENLY —
HALT! WHO GOES THERE?
ROBBERS!
WE HAVE NO MONEY. PLEASE LET US GO.
HA! HA! YOU CANNOT DECEIVE US WITH HUMBLE TALK AND SIMPLE CLOTHES! IF YOU ARE CARRYING NO MONEY, YOUR PUPIL CAN BRING IT FROM YOUR HOUSE.
THEY BOUND THE PANDIT TO A TREE.
RUN FAST AND BRING A THOUSAND GOLD COINS. ONLY THEN WILL YOUR GURU BE FREED!

MASTER, I'LL COME BACK AS SOON AS POSSIBLE. SO PLEASE DO NOT TELL THESE THUGS THAT YOU KNOW THE VAIDARBHA MANTRA !
THE VAIDARBHA MANTRA IS A CHANT KNOWN TO VERY FEW. IF UTTERED WHEN THE STARS ARE IN A FAVOURABLE POSITION, IT PRODUCES A SHOWER OF GEMS.
NOW HURRY UP, BOY, AND DO WHAT YOU'VE BEEN TOLD !
I'LL COME BACK WITH THE MONEY IN TWO DAYS.
THAT NIGHT —
HOW COLD IT IS ! ALL MY JOINTS ACHE ! I WISH I COULD WARM MYSELF NEAR THAT FIRE. BUT THEY WILL KEEP ME TIED TO THIS TREE TILL MY PUPIL RETURNS !
THE PANDIT LOOKED UP AT THE SKY —
OH ! THE PLANETS ARE MOVING INTO THE CORRECT POSITION. SHOULD I TELL THE ROBBERS ABOUT THE VAIDARBHA MANTRA AND SO BE FREE AGAIN ?

REMEMBERING HIS PUPIL'S ADVICE, HE HESITATED. BUT FINALLY —
AFTER ALL, WHAT IS THE USE OF KNOWLEDGE IF ONE CANNOT UTILISE IT IN TIMES OF CRISIS ?
HEY, CHIEF! LISTEN! I HAVE SOMETHING IMPORTANT TO SAY!
IF I START A SHOWER OF GEMS, WILL YOU LET ME GO ?
A SHOWER OF GEMS ? ARE YOU JOKING ?
NO, I'M SERIOUS. I CAN DO IT BY MEANS OF A MAGIC CHANT.
BUT...!
IN A FEW MOMENTS THE PLANETS WILL BE IN THE RIGHT POSITION. THEN I CAN BEGIN.
ALL RIGHT, GO AHEAD!

I CAN'T DO IT WITHOUT HAVING A RITUAL BATH AND CHANGING INTO CLEAN SILK CLOTHES...
...AND, OF COURSE, YOU WILL FIRST HAVE TO SET ME FREE!
ALL RIGHT. BUT DON'T PLAY ANY TRICKS OR IT WILL BE THE WORSE FOR YOU!
SO THE PANDIT WAS SET FREE, AND AFTER A DIP IN THE RIVER, HE SAT FOR A LONG TIME, RECITING THE CHANT.
CAN HE REALLY DO IT, OR IS HE FOOLING US?
WILL IT HAPPEN?
HOW LONG WILL IT TAKE?
FINALLY, HE FINISHED.
THE VERY NEXT MOMENT —
GEMS! THOSE ARE PRECIOUS GEMS FALLING DOWN!

QUICK! COLLECT THEM ALL! EVEN THE TINIEST!
GOOD WORK! YOU ARE FREE TO GO NOW.
IT IS A GOOD THING I DIDN'T LISTEN TO MY PUPIL.
BUT, THE NEXT MOMENT —
STAY WHERE YOU ARE! YOU ARE SURROUNDED!
TIE THEM ALL UP!
WAIT! FIRST TELL ME WHY YOU ARE DOING THIS!
WHAT A STUPID QUESTION! FOR YOUR GEMS, OF COURSE.
IS THAT ALL? THEN YOU NEED ONLY TO TAKE CHARGE OF THIS PANDIT HERE.
ANY MORE JOKES FROM YOU, AND YOU'LL BE HUNG UP FROM THE NEAREST TREE!

OF WHAT USE COULD THAT KNOCK-KNEED PANDIT BE TO ME ?
HE'S INVALUABLE! HE KNOWS A MAGIC CHANT THAT WILL BRING DOWN A SHOWER OF JEWELS. THAT'S HOW WE CAME BY OURS!
OH, IN THAT CASE, WE WILL SET YOU FREE AND KEEP ONLY THE PANDIT !
THE CHIEF OF THE SECOND GANG TURNED TO THE PANDIT.
MY FRIEND, LET'S HAVE A BIG SHOWER OF GEMS!
YOU SHALL HAVE IT — BUT ONLY AFTER ONE YEAR.
DON'T MAKE A FOOL OF ME. I WANT THE JEWELS NOW !
I... I'M... SORRY. THE CHANT IS EFFECTIVE ONLY AT A SPECIFIC TIME. THE AUSPICIOUS MOMENT WILL NOT OCCUR AGAIN FOR ANOTHER YEAR.
LIAR ! SCOUNDREL ! WE WON'T LET YOU GET AWAY WITH IT.

BELIEVE ME! IT IS FUTILE! I CAN'T HELP YOU!
YOU WANT TO TRICK US? DO YOU THINK WE ARE FOOLS?
HAVE MERCY!... OH... OH... GOD!... HELP!
IF ONLY I HAD LISTENED TO MY PUPIL'S ADVICE!
COME ON, LET'S GO AFTER THOSE RASCALS WE SET FREE! THEY'VE TRICKED US, BUT THEY WON'T GO FAR WITH THOSE GEMS!
HEY! STOP!
IT'S THE OTHER GANG OF ROBBERS AGAIN!

A FIERCE FIGHT ENSUED...
... AND THE FIRST GANG WAS VANQUISHED —
NOW THE GEMS ARE MINE!
NO, MINE!
MINE!
YOU RASCAL, TAKE THAT!
SUDDENLY —
CHIEF! LOOK! HE IS RIDING AWAY WITH THE GEMS!
HEY! YOU! STOP!

AH! I'VE GOT IT!
NO, MY FRIEND! IT IS MINE!
HEY! GIVE IT BACK!
AFTER SOME TIME —
WHAT? ONLY TWO OF US LEFT!
LET'S STOP FIGHTING AND SHARE THE BOOTY.
REALISING IT WAS USELESS TO FIGHT, THEY PRETENDED TO BE FRIENDS. THEY HID THE TREASURE IN THE HOLLOW OF A TREE.
I AM FEELING HUNGRY. LET'S GO AND EAT.
ONE OF US SHOULD STAY HERE TO GUARD THE TREASURE.
ALL RIGHT, I'LL GO AND FETCH SOME FOOD WHILE YOU KEEP GUARD HERE.
BUT DO RETURN SOON — I AM FAMISHED!
WHY SHOULD I SHARE THE TREASURE WITH HIM? HE DOESN'T DESERVE IT.

I'LL HIDE BEHIND THIS ROCK AND SURPRISE HIM WHEN HE COMES BACK.
MEANWHILE, THE OTHER ROBBER WENT TO THE VILLAGE NEAR BY AND BOUGHT SOME FOOD. ON HIS WAY BACK —
I'M STARVING. I'LL EAT FIRST AND THEN TAKE THE REST FOR MY FRIEND.
BUT, REALLY, HE IS NO FRIEND OF MINE AT ALL. WHY SHOULD I SHARE ANYTHING WITH HIM ?
I WILL SHARE NEITHER FOOD NOR JEWELS WITH HIM. I'LL GET RID OF HIM!
SO HE SPRINKLED SOME POISON ON THE REMAINING FOOD.
THEN HE SET OFF AGAIN.
THIS WILL TAKE CARE OF HIM!

BUT WHEN HE ARRIVED —
THE TREASURE IS ALL MINE NOW!
AAH!
AND NOW, FOR SOME FOOD. AH! I AM AS RICH AS A KING TODAY!
BUT IT WAS ALL IN VAIN. FOR, HAVING EATEN THE POISONED FOOD, HE, TOO, FELL DEAD.
WHEN, TWO DAYS LATER, THE PUPIL RETURNED WITH THE MONEY, HE FOUND THE PLACE LITTERED WITH CORPSES.
MY GURU USED THE CHANT FOR THE BENEFIT OF UNDESERV-ING PEOPLE! IF ONLY HE HAD HEEDED MY ADVICE!

THE DRUMMER
A DRUMMER AND HIS SON ONCE WENT TO VARANASI TO PLAY AT A FESTIVAL.
AT THE END OF THE FESTIVAL —
HERE IS SOME MONEY FOR BOTH OF YOU. YOUR SON IS A VERY GOOD DRUMMER.
AND HERE ARE SOME JEWELS.
AND SOME CLOTHES.
FATHER, I ENJOYED THE FESTIVAL VERY MUCH.
YOU GAVE A GOOD PERFORMANCE, SON.
THE NEXT MOMENT —
WHAT ARE YOU DOING?
BEATING THE DRUM — WHAT ELSE? I FEEL ON TOP OF THE WORLD TODAY, FATHER!

DON'T MAKE SUCH A DIN! YOU WILL ATTRACT ROBBERS! THIS FOREST IS FULL OF THEM!
I'LL PLAY A MARTIAL BEAT TO FRIGHTEN THEM OFF, FATHER!
SOME THIEVES HIDING IN THE JUNGLE HEARD THE LOUD DRUMMING.
IT APPEARS A ROYAL PARTY IS HUNTING IN THE FOREST.
AFTER A WHILE —
ENOUGH, SON! DON'T DO IT AGAIN! THAT SHOULD ONLY BE PLAYED ONCE!
BUT THE BOY WENT ON —
STOP! WHY DON'T YOU LISTEN TO ME?
OH, FATHER, YOU WORRY TOO MUCH! I'LL SCARE THE THIEVES GOOD AND PROPER!
WHAT! THE SAME DRUM-BEATS THRICE! THAT IS NO ROYAL PARTY.
IT IS JUST SOMEBODY WHO HAS MADE A LOT OF MONEY AND IS FEELING HAPPY!
LET'S ATTACK HIM!

THE THIEVES QUICKLY SPOTTED THE DRUMMER AND HIS SON.
OH, YES! THOSE TWO CERTAINLY HAVE SOME MONEY IN THOSE HEAVY BUNDLES!

STOP! DON'T MOVE!
GIVE US ALL YOU HAVE!

WHAT A LOVELY NECKLACE!
THE CLOTHES ARE NEW, TOO.
AND THE THIEVES RAN OFF WITH THE LOOT.

I TOLD YOU TO STOP, DIDN'T I? BUT YOU WOULDN'T LISTEN. IN YOUR PRIDE, YOU FOOLISHLY INVITED YOUR OWN DOOM BY PLAYING AT THE WRONG TIME!
I HAVE LEARNT MY LESSON NOW, FATHER!

THE SADHU AND THE RAM
ONE DAY, THERE WAS GREAT EXCITEMENT IN VARANASI. PEOPLE HAD GATHERED TO WATCH A RAM-FIGHT.
A SADHU HAPPENED TO PASS BY.
WHAT IS GOING ON?
A RAM-FIGHT! OH, WHAT FINE BEASTS THEY ARE!
THE SADHU PUSHED HIS WAY IN.
HE SAW A RAM RETREATING WITH HIS HEAD BOWED LOW.
HE IS STEPPING BACK! HE IS BOWING BEFORE ME!
O, NOBLE BEAST! ONLY YOU, IN THIS WHOLE CROWD OF PEOPLE, KNOW A GREAT SOUL WHEN YOU SEE ONE!

A MAN IN THE CROWD CALLED OUT IN WARNING —
BE CAREFUL! HE IS NOT BOWING BEFORE YOU...!
...HE IS PREPARING TO ATTACK! PLEASE STEP BACK!
NO, I WON'T! THE POOR ANIMAL WANTS ME TO BLESS HIM!
A MOMENT LATER —
A-A-H!
I HAVE INVITED THIS AGONY ON MYSELF! I WAS FOOLISH AND VAIN! NOW I HAVE PAID THE PRICE!

THE DAY THE EARTH BROKE INTO TWO
ONE DAY A RABBIT WAS RELAXING UNDER A BILVA TREE ...
... WHEN A STRANGE THOUGHT STRUCK HIM —
I WONDER WHAT WILL HAPPEN IF THE EARTH BREAKS INTO TWO?
JUST THEN, A BILVA FRUIT FELL FROM THE TREE ...
THUD
WH... WHAT IS THAT?
... AND ROLLED OVER DRY PALM LEAVES.
IS THE EARTH REALLY GOING TO BREAK? I MUST RUN AWAY TO A SAFE PLACE!

WHAT'S THE MATTER? WHERE ARE YOU GOING?
DON'T ASK ME, BROTHER. JUST RUN FOR YOUR LIFE!
THE SECOND RABBIT FOLLOWED THE FIRST ONE.
BUT WHY? WHAT'S HAPPENED?
OH! THE EARTH IS ABOUT TO BREAK!
VERY SOON, A HORDE OF FRIGHTENED RABBITS WERE RUNNING. THEN —
WHAT HAS HAPPENED? WHY THE PANIC? I'LL ASK THEM.
LEARNING THAT THE EARTH WAS GOING TO BREAK, THE DEER ALSO JOINED THE RABBITS.
HEY, WHERE ARE YOU ALL GOING? WHAT IS THE HURRY?
DON'T YOU KNOW? THE EARTH IS BREAKING...!
THE EARTH... IS BREAKING? THEN I MUST SAVE MYSELF TOO!

VERY SOON A PANIC-STRICKEN TROUPE WAS FLEEING THROUGH THE FOREST.
THEN A LION CAME BY ——
WHAT'S GOING ON HERE?
OH, DON'T YOU KNOW? THE EARTH IS BREAKING!
HMM.... BUT THAT IS IMPOSSIBLE!
HE CLIMBED TO THE TOP OF A HILL AND ROARED.
GR-GR-GR-GR

THE ANIMALS FROZE IN THEIR TRACKS.
WHY ARE YOU RUNNING? WHAT IS THE MATTER?
THE EARTH IS BREAKING, O MIGHTY ONE!
WE MUST GO AWAY FROM HERE!
WHO SAW THIS HAPPEN?
THE ELEPHANT. ASK HIM!
NO, NO. NOT ME. ASK THE TIGER.
OH, NO! THE PANTHER REPORTED IT TO ME. ASK HIM!
FINALLY, THE RABBIT WAS BROUGHT TO THE LION.
DID YOU REALLY SEE THE EARTH BREAKING, LITTLE ONE?
YES, MY LORD. I SAW IT WITH MY OWN EYES.
TELL ME, WHERE WAS THIS?
IT WAS NEAR MY BURROW WHICH IS UNDER A BILVA TREE IN A PALM GROVE.

I WAS JUST LYING DOWN THERE WONDERING WHAT I WOULD DO IF THE EARTH WERE TO BREAK, WHEN SUDDENLY...
... IT HAPPENED! I HEARD A DEAFENING NOISE AND FLED.
A PALM GROVE... A BILVA TREE... HMM.... I AM SURE HE HAS MADE A MISTAKE.
I'LL GO WITH THE RABBIT AND FIND OUT WHAT REALLY HAPPENED. WAIT HERE TILL I COME BACK.
VERY WELL, O MIGHTY ONE!
AND THE LION WENT OFF WITH THE RABBIT.

WHEN THEY REACHED THE PALM GROVE —
SHOW ME THE PLACE WHERE YOU HEARD THE NOISE. DON'T BE AFRAID. I'M HERE TO PROTECT YOU.
THAT'S THE BILVA TREE WHERE I HEARD THE THUNDERING NOISE!
ALL RIGHT. YOU WAIT FOR ME HERE. I'LL GO AND LOOK AROUND.
THE LION LOOKED CLOSELY AT THE PALM LEAVES UNDERNEATH THE BILVA TREE.
AH! JUST AS I THOUGHT! THE SOUND OF THE FRUIT FALLING ON DRY LEAVES FRIGHTENED THE RABBIT AND HE THOUGHT THAT THE EARTH WAS BREAKING.
RETURNING TO THE WAITING ANIMALS, THE LION TOLD THEM WHAT HE HAD DISCOVERED.
FRIENDS, YOU DID NOT CHECK IF THIS WAS TRUE. BLINDLY RELYING ON A FALSE RUMOUR, YOU WOULD HAVE PAID A HEAVY PRICE TODAY.

THE FOOLISH TREE

I CAN'T BEAR IT ANY LONGER! I'LL DRIVE THESE ANIMALS AWAY.
OH, NO! PLEASE DON'T! THE WILD ANIMALS PROTECT US, AND KEEP MEN AWAY!

BUT JUST IMAGINE, HOW PURE AND PLEASANT THE AIR WILL BE!

I'LL DO IT! I'LL DRIVE THEM AWAY!
OH, MY FRIEND! YOU DON'T KNOW WHAT YOU ARE DOING!

ONE NIGHT, SHORTLY AFTERWARDS —
AH! A STRONG BREEZE IS BLOWING THIS WAY. HERE IS MY CHANCE!

THE TREE SHOOK ITSELF VIGOROUSLY, MAKING A LOUD NOISE...
SHR-SHR-SHR-SHR!
...WHICH AWAKENED THE ANIMALS SLEEPING BENEATH IT.
WHAT'S HAPPENING?
LOOK AT THAT TREE!
HOW IT IS SWAYING!
THE TREE IS POSSESSED!
LET'S RUN AWAY!
YES, ALL OF US HAD BETTER LEAVE!
HURRY!
THE NEXT MORNING —
AT LAST, I'VE GOT RID OF THOSE ANIMALS! ALREADY, THE AIR SMELLS FRESHER!

MANY DAYS PASSED. QUIET AND PEACE REIGNED IN THE FOREST. THEN ONE AFTERNOON, A COWHERD PASSED THAT WAY.
SH...O...O... COME BACK, YOU NAUGHTY ONE! THE LION WILL EAT YOU UP!
FOLLOWING THE CALF, THE BOY VENTURED INTO THE FOREST.
I HOPE A TIGER DOESN'T POUNCE ON ME!
BUT THERE SEEM TO BE NO TIGERS HERE! AND NO ANIMAL FOOTPRINTS ANYWHERE AROUND!
HE WENT HOME AND TOLD HIS FAMILY ABOUT THIS DISCOVERY. THE NEXT DAY —
IT LOOKS AS IF NO ANIMALS HAVE LIVED HERE FOR AGES!
HE IS RIGHT!
THIS LAND COULD BE VERY USEFUL TO US.

YOU SEE WHAT THEY ARE PLANNING? I HAD TOLD YOU TO LET THE WILD BEASTS ALONE.
DON'T BE SILLY. I CAN FRIGHTEN THOSE MEN AWAY, AS I DID THE BEASTS!
THE TREE SHOOK ITSELF VIOLENTLY, MAKING A LOUD SOUND —
SHR... SHR... S
WHAT IS THAT AWFUL SOUND, FATHER?
IT'S NOTHING, SON! JUST THE BREEZE, RUSTLING THROUGH THE LEAVES!
THE TREE TRIED AGAIN.
SHR... SHI
HEY! WATCH OUT!

OH! IT'S NOTHING TO WORRY ABOUT! JUST A FEW TWIGS HAVE FALLEN DOWN! WE'LL CUT DOWN THESE TREES. THE WOOD WILL COME IN USEFUL.
SOON THE FOREST WAS FULL OF PEOPLE FROM THE VILLAGE NEAR BY.
JUST A FEW MORE STROKES, BROTHER!
YES, THEN THE TREE WILL FALL DOWN.
WE'LL TACKLE THIS TREE TOMORROW.
THEY'RE POINTING TO ME! WHAT SHALL I DO?
THAT NIGHT —
HELP, FRIEND! HELP ME, PLEASE! YOU HEARD THEM, DIDN'T YOU? THEY ARE COMING FOR ME TOMORROW!
IT IS TOO LATE! NOW YOU MUST BEAR THE CONSEQUENCES OF YOUR ACTION!
AND THAT WAS THE END OF THE TREE.

THE LOST GRAM
ONCE A KING AND HIS ARMY HAD ENCAMPED OUTSIDE A CITY.
A MONKEY WATCHED THEM CLOSELY FROM A TREE.
I HAVE BEEN FEELING HUNGRY ALL DAY BUT NOW IT APPEARS I'LL HAVE A FEAST!
A LITTLE LATER —
LET'S ROAST SOME GRAM FOR THE HORSES.
HA! JUST AS I EXPECTED. HOW LUCKY I AM!
WE'LL FEED THE HORSES WHEN THE GRAM GETS COLD.
THIS IS MY CHANCE!
AS THE SOLDIERS TURNED TO LEAVE, THE MONKEY SWOOPED DOWN FROM THE TREE...

... AND ATE A HANDFUL OF GRAM.
THIS IS DELICIOUS!
BUT THOUGH HIS HUNGER WAS SATISFIED, HIS GREED WAS NOT.
I MUST TAKE AWAY AS MUCH AS I CAN!
HE STUFFED HIS MOUTH WITH GRAM...
... AND GRABBED SOME MORE WITH BOTH FRONT PAWS.
I'LL HAVE ENOUGH FOR MANY MORE DAYS!
HA! NOW I'LL EAT SOME MORE!
BUT ONE GRAIN ROLLED OUT AND...
...FELL ON THE GROUND.
OH... OH, MY GRAM! IT'S GONE!

I WON'T ALLOW THIS! I MUST GET IT BACK!
WITHOUT THINKING, HE THREW AWAY ALL THE GRAM HE HAD AND...
...SPRANG DOWN TO LOOK FOR THE ONE FALLEN GRAIN.
IT MUST BE SOMEWHERE AROUND HERE!
WHERE COULD IT HAVE GONE?
I CAN'T FIND IT ANYWHERE!
AND, ALAS, I HAVE LOST THE REST OF THE GRAM TOO!
THUS, THE FOOLISH MONKEY, IN BEING NIGGARDLY ABOUT ONE GRAIN OF GRAM, LOST ALL HE HAD.

BUT...BUT!
AAAH!
I AM A FOOL. I WISH I COULD PROVE MYSELF TO BE CLEVER.
THAT IS BECAUSE...